Kenai

Denahi

Sitka

Rutt

Tuke

Published by Scholastic Inc., 90 Old Sherman Turnpike, Danbury, Connecticut 06816.

ISBN 0-7172-6823-3

Printed in the U.S.A.
First printing, November 2003

SCHOLASTIC INC.

New York   Toronto   London   Auckland   Sydney
Mexico City   New Delhi   Hong Kong   Buenos Aires

Long ago, there lived three
brothers who were taught that the
lights of the northern sky were
the spirits of their ancestors.
These spirits had the power
to make changes—small
things into big, winter
into spring, and boys
into men. . . .

One day, the villagers gathered for a special ceremony. Tanana, the shaman woman, presented Kenai, the youngest of the three brothers, with his totem—the animal symbol he was to follow to become a man.

"Your totem is love," said Tanana, giving him a carved bear totem. "Let love guide your actions, and one day, you will place your mark next to those of our ancestors," she added, pointing to a wall covered with handprints.

"The bear of love?" Kenai frowned. "Wanna trade?" he asked his brothers.

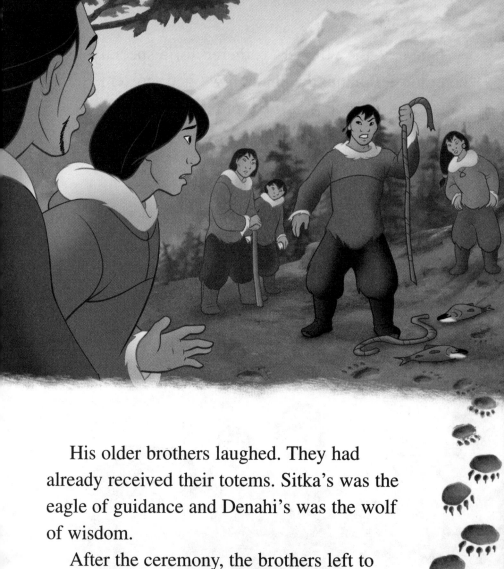

His older brothers laughed. They had
already received their totems. Sitka's was the
eagle of guidance and Denahi's was the wolf
of wisdom.

After the ceremony, the brothers left to
get the fish they had caught for the evening's
feast. "A bear doesn't love anyone," Kenai
said unhappily to Sitka. "They don't think,
they don't feel, they're—"

Just then Denahi found the remains of
the basket that had held their fish. "Thieves!"
shouted Kenai, staring at the bear tracks.

Kenai followed the tracks into the woods to find the basket.

When Kenai didn't return, Sitka and Denahi went after him. It wasn't long before they heard Kenai cry out. He had slipped off a ledge trying to escape from a bear!

Quickly Denahi distracted the bear while Sitka helped Kenai. But then Denahi slipped into a dangerous crevice. While Kenai helped him, Sitka faced the bear.

Suddenly the bear turned and headed for Kenai and Denahi. To save his brothers, Sitka raised his spear and thrust it down into a crack in the ice. The ice split, and the piece on which Sitka and the bear were standing plunged into the freezing water below.

From far above, Kenai and Denahi saw the bear emerge from the water—but not Sitka. Their oldest brother would now be joining the Great Spirits in the form of his totem—the eagle. Denahi felt great sadness. But Kenai felt great anger!

The next day, Kenai was determined to go after the bear that had caused Sitka's death. But Denahi would not go with him. Angry, Kenai threw his bear totem into a fire and left the village.

Tanana pulled the totem from the fire.

"I've got to go after him," Denahi said, taking the bear totem.

Kenai tracked and eventually found the bear. After a fierce struggle, Kenai fell to the ground. The animal charged towards him. Kenai raised his spear. The bear crashed into him, let out a roar, and then fell silent.

Suddenly lights burst down from the sky and swirled around Kenai. A giant eagle landed next to him and turned into Sitka. Then Kenai felt himself being lifted into the air. He didn't realize that he was being magically transformed into the creature he hated most—a bear!

The lights disappeared and it began to rain.

Just then Denahi arrived and saw a grizzly bear standing on Kenai's clothes. Denahi didn't know Kenai was now a bear. So he thought that the bear had killed Kenai. Before he could react, a bolt of lightning sent the bear tumbling into the river below. Kenai was swept away.

Now it was Denahi's turn to want revenge. He tied Kenai's bear totem to his spear and began to track the bear.

When Kenai opened his eyes the next morning, Tanana was leaning over him.

Kenai spoke to her excitedly, telling her all that had happened to him. But all Tanana could hear were growls.

"Kenai, I don't speak bear!" said the wise woman.

Kenai didn't understand. Then he looked into the river at his reflection. "No!" he shouted. He twisted around and looked at his furry tail. "AAAHHH!" he cried.

To get Kenai's attention, Tanana took off her boot
and bonked him on the head with it. "Listen to me!
Sitka did this!" said Tanana. "Take it up with your
brother's spirit! If you want to change, go to the
mountain where the lights touch the earth.
He'll help you make up for what you've
done wrong."

Kenai was shocked. "But . . . I didn't do
anything wrong," he
began. But Tanana
had already
disappeared.

Kenai didn't know where to go, and he
had no one to ask—until he heard two chipmunks
talking. Kenai was surprised he could understand them.
He tried to talk to them, but the terrified chipmunks
raced away.

Then Kenai heard a family of geese flying overhead.
"Are we there yet?" a young goose asked his father.

Kenai frantically tried
asking for directions
to where the
lights touch the
earth, but the geese
kept flying.

Two moose brothers named Rutt and
Tuke were watching Kenai.

"What's he getting all worked up about?"
said the moose named Tuke.

"Maybe the goose pooped on him, eh?"
said Rutt, laughing.

But the moose
stopped laughing when
they saw that the
bear was headed
for them.

"How's it going, bear?" asked Tuke, a little nervously.

"I'm not a bear. I hate bears," answered Kenai.

"Well, gee, you're one big beaver!" said Rutt.

"I'm NOT a beaver! I'm a bear. No, I mean I'm not a bear, I'm a man!" Kenai shouted. "I was transformed into a bear. Magically."

The moose thought Kenai was crazy and decided to play along.

"Oh, yeah, we're not moose either. We're . . . squirrels," Tuke offered.

"Why am I even talking to a couple of dumb moose?" Kenai wondered, as he stomped off.

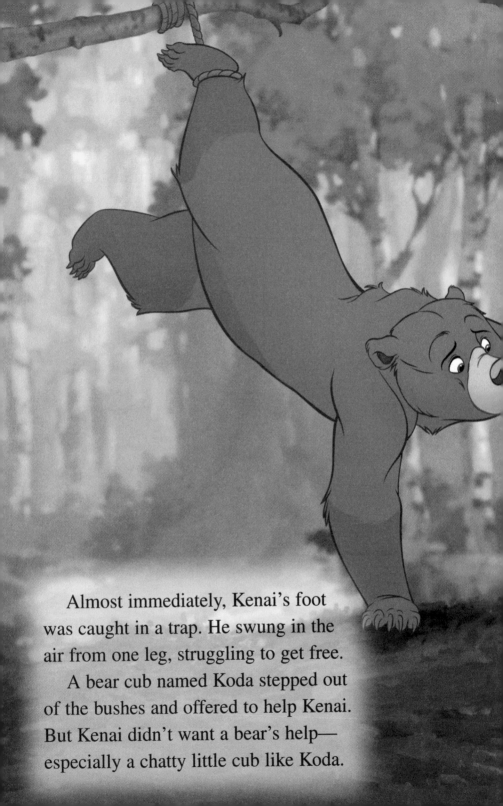

Almost immediately, Kenai's foot
was caught in a trap. He swung in the
air from one leg, struggling to get free.
    A bear cub named Koda stepped out
of the bushes and offered to help Kenai.
But Kenai didn't want a bear's help—
especially a chatty little cub like Koda.

Kenai tried to free himself, but it was no use. And Koda just wouldn't leave.

"Don't you have somewhere to go?" asked Kenai.

"Yeah, the Salmon Run," answered Koda. "How about this? I get you down. Then we go together?"

Kenai was so exhausted that he agreed to go to the Salmon Run if Koda would free him.

With that, Koda sprang the trap and Kenai crashed to the ground.

Just then Koda sniffed the air. He could smell an approaching hunter! "Run!" he cried, as he scampered off.

The hunter was Denahi!

Kenai cried, "Denahi, it's me—Kenai!"

But all Denahi heard was growling. To Denahi, this was the bear that had killed Kenai. He threw his spear, but missed.

Kenai realized Denahi was hunting him and ran away.

Kenai ducked into the same ice cave where Koda was hiding. Kenai told the little bear that he wasn't going to go to the Salmon Run.

So Koda told Kenai the truth: A hunter had caused him and his mother to be separated. Koda's only hope of finding her was to go to the Salmon Run. Still, Kenai refused to go.

"C'mon, please? Every night we watch the lights touch the mountain," pleaded Koda.

"You're kidding me!" said Kenai excitedly. That was the place where he could be changed back into a man! Kenai agreed to go with the little cub.

The next morning, the two bears set out.
At first Kenai was annoyed by
Koda's constant chatter and
silly games. But after a
while, Kenai joined in
and even had some fun.

Once again, Rutt and Tuke appeared. "There's a hunter followin' us," Rutt explained. The two moose wanted the bears to protect them.

Kenai knew the hunter was Denahi. And he had a plan to keep Denahi from following their tracks. The group, along with some other animals, found a herd of mammoths and hitched a ride on their backs.

That night, as they watched the lights in the northern sky, Koda said, "Mom says the spirits make magical changes in the world."

"My brother Sitka is a spirit," explained Kenai. "If it wasn't for him, I wouldn't be here." Then Kenai added, "He was killed by a monster."

Koda looked up at the lights and said, "Thanks, Sitka. If it weren't for you, I would have never met Kenai." Then Koda said to Kenai, "I always wanted a brother." Touched, Kenai let the cub sleep next to him.

The next morning, the two bears headed off by themselves. They came to a cave covered with paintings. As they looked at one painting of a hunter facing a fierce bear, Koda said, "Those monsters are really scary—especially with those sticks."

Kenai was shocked to learn Koda saw humans as monsters. Kenai had thought the bears were the monsters. But now Kenai wasn't sure what he believed.

Later, the two bears came to a valley with spurting geysers. Koda remembered that the Salmon Run was just on the other side. As they made their way through the valley, the little bear was as playful as ever. But suddenly Koda stopped playing.

THWACK! A spear just missed Kenai by inches! Denahi had found them!

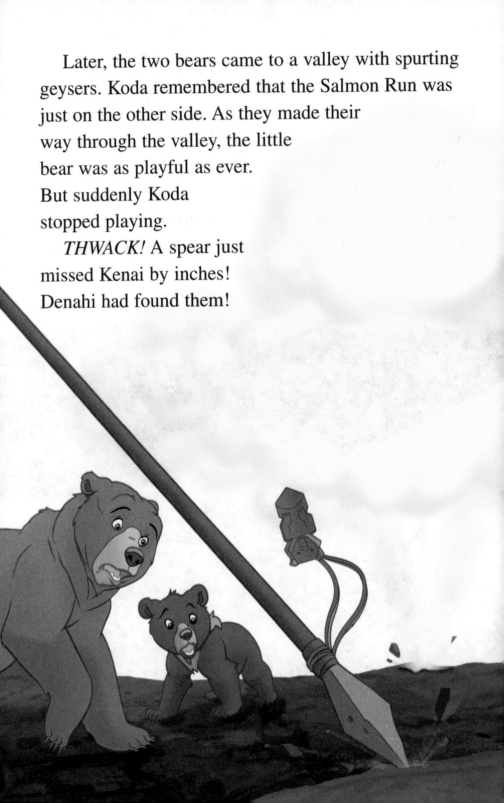

Kenai grabbed Koda and rushed towards a log bridge. They were halfway across the bridge when Denahi cut the log loose. Kenai tossed Koda up to safe ground, then scrambled to safety just as the bridge collapsed.

Denahi screamed in rage as the bears got away. When Kenai looked back, he felt very sad that his brother did not know him.

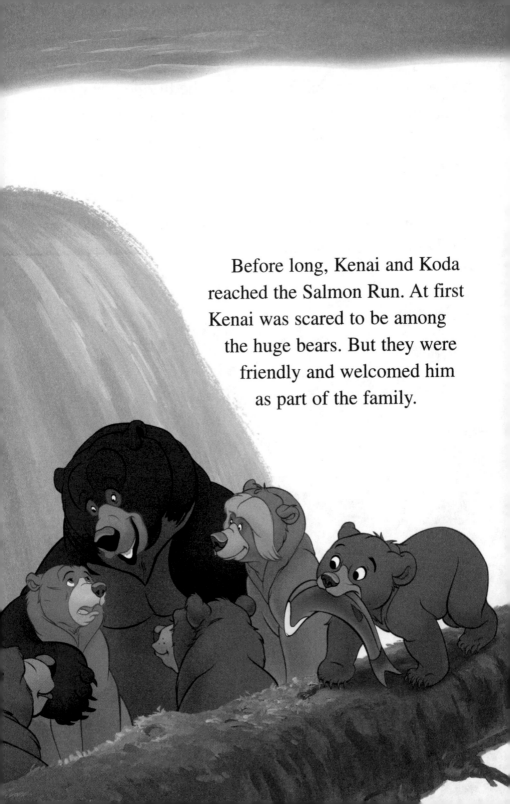

Before long, Kenai and Koda
reached the Salmon Run. At first
Kenai was scared to be among
the huge bears. But they were
friendly and welcomed him
as part of the family.

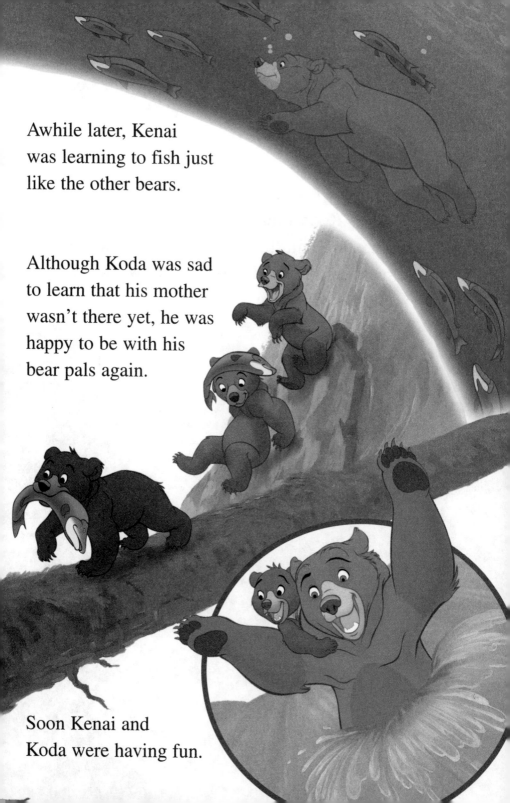

Awhile later, Kenai
was learning to fish just
like the other bears.

Although Koda was sad
to learn that his mother
wasn't there yet, he was
happy to be with his
bear pals again.

Soon Kenai and
Koda were having fun.

Later in the day, the bears gathered around to tell stories of what they had done in the past year. Kenai explained that he'd been on the hardest journey of his life with the biggest pain in the neck he had ever met. "But what do you expect from a little brother?" Kenai added, looking at Koda.

Then it was Koda's turn. He told a story of his mother protecting him from some hunters. She and one of the hunters had plunged into the river when the hunter had cracked the ice.

Kenai couldn't believe what he was hearing. Koda
was telling the story of the day his brother Sitka was
killed by a bear. Now he knew it was also the story of
a mother bear protecting her cub.

"She got out of the water okay," continued Koda.
"That's how we got separated. Right after that,
I met Kenai."

Hearing this, Kenai realized that the bear he had
killed was Koda's mother! Kenai felt terrible.

Kenai felt so badly that he ran away. But Koda finally found him. Kenai knew he had to tell the cub the truth.

"Koda," Kenai began, "I have a story to tell you . . . it's mostly about a monster." Then Kenai explained he had done something very wrong. "Your mother's not coming back," he finished sadly.

Overwhelmed by the news, Koda ran away from Kenai.

Having no way to make things better, Kenai began to climb the mountain where the lights touch the earth.

After he reached the top, Kenai called for Sitka. A strange figure moved towards Kenai. It was Denahi! But Denahi did not see his brother Kenai. What he saw was the bear on whom he had sworn revenge. Denahi ran at Kenai with his spear.

Just then Koda came charging
to protect Kenai. The little cub
had decided to follow Kenai after
all. He knocked into Denahi and
ran off with his spear. Denahi
angrily took off after Koda.

"Leave him alone!" roared Kenai,
risking his own life to protect Koda.

Suddenly there was a large flash of light.

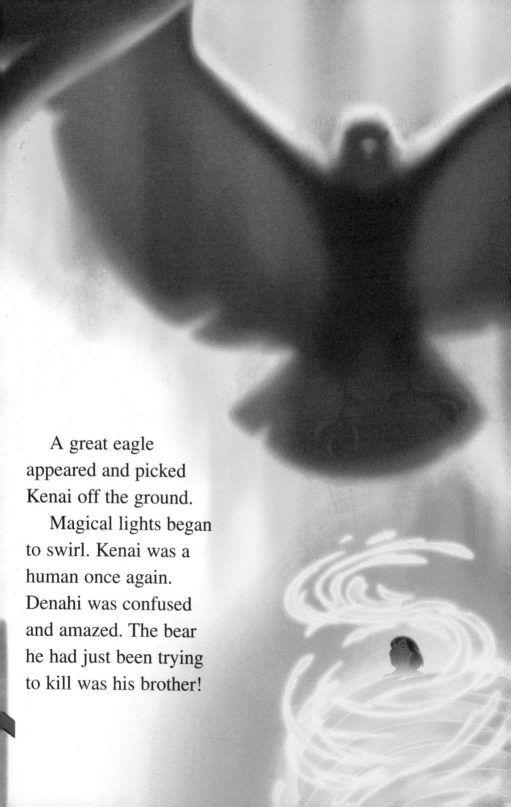

A great eagle
appeared and picked
Kenai off the ground.
    Magical lights began
to swirl. Kenai was a
human once again.
Denahi was confused
and amazed. The bear
he had just been trying
to kill was his brother!

The eagle spirit of Sitka had turned Kenai into a bear to help him learn his gift of love. As a bear, Kenai had just demonstrated a deep love for Koda. He was willing to give his own life to protect him.

Awestruck, Kenai looked down at his human body as Sitka changed from an eagle to his human spirit form.

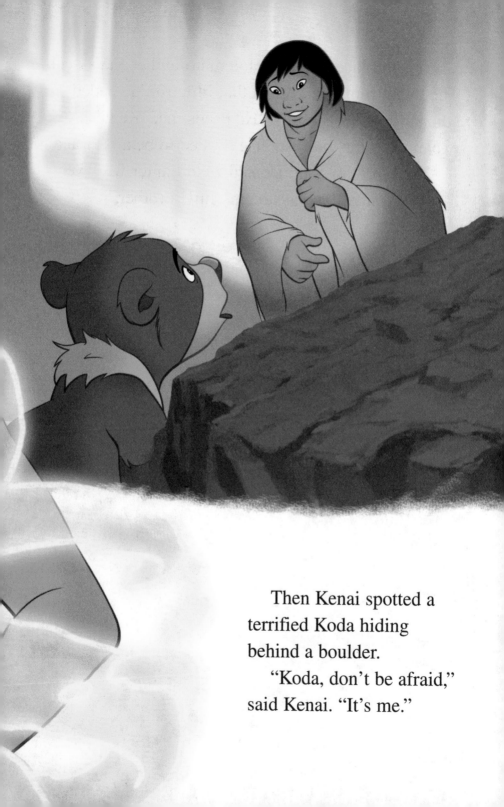

Then Kenai spotted a
terrified Koda hiding
behind a boulder.

"Koda, don't be afraid,"
said Kenai. "It's me."

Denahi placed the bear totem around Kenai's neck. The totem reminded Kenai that little Koda needed someone to protect him. "He needs me," Kenai explained to his brothers. He wanted to be a bear again.

"It's all right," said Denahi. "No matter what you choose, you will always be my little brother."

The two brothers embraced.
Then with a burst of swirling
light, Sitka turned Kenai
back into a bear again.

Denahi looked up
at his brother, who
was now an
enormous bear.
"Did I say *little?*"

Then Kenai,
Denahi, and Koda
watched the sky as
Sitka turned into an eagle
and flew back into the magical
lights to join the Great Spirits.

It was time for another ceremony in the village. It was Kenai's turn to put his mark on the ceremonial wall to prove that he had learned the way of his totem and was now an adult.

With Koda and the villagers watching, Denahi helped Kenai place his paw print on the wall among

the handprints of their ancestors.
    The paw print would help
future generations remember
this tale of love and
brotherhood.